Alfie Gives a Hand

Also by Shirley Hughes
ALFIE'S FEET
ALFIE GETS IN FIRST

Library of Congress Cataloging in Publication Data
Hughes, Shirley.
    Alfie gives a hand.
    Summary: Holding tightly to his old bit of blanket as he attends his first
birthday party, Alfie finds a way to be helpful, but it means putting down his
blanket first.
    [1. Parties—Fiction.   2. Blankets—Fiction.   3. Helpfulness—Fiction.]
I. Title.
PZ7.H87395 Ald 1983   [E]   83-14883
ISBN 0-688-06521-X

Alfie Gives a Hand

Shirley Hughes

MULBERRY BOOKS · New York

One day Alfie came home from nursery
school with a card in an envelope. His best
friend, Bernard, had given it to him.

"Look, it's got my name on it," said
Alfie, pointing.

"It's an invitation to Bernard's birthday
party," said Mom.

"Will it be at Bernard's house?" Alfie wanted to know. He'd never been there before. Mom said yes, and she told him all about birthday parties, and how you had to take a present, and about the games and how there would be nice things to eat.

Alfie was very excited about Bernard's party. When the day came Mom washed Alfie's face and brushed his hair and helped him put on a clean T-shirt and his brand-new shorts.

"You and Annie Rose are going to be at the party too, aren't you?" asked Alfie.

"Oh, no," said Mom. "I'll take you to Bernard's house, and then Annie Rose and I will go to the park and come back to collect you when it's time to go home."

"But I want you to be there," said Alfie.

Mom told him that she and Annie Rose hadn't been invited to the party, only Alfie, because he was Bernard's special friend.

"You don't mind my leaving you at nursery school, do you?" she said. "So you won't mind being at Bernard's house either, as soon as you get there."

Mom had bought some crayons for Alfie to give Bernard for his birthday present. While she was wrapping them up, Alfie went upstairs. He looked under his pillow and found his old bit of blanket, which he kept in bed with him at night.

He brought it downstairs and sat down to wait for Mom.

"You won't want your old blanket at the party," said Mom when it was time to go.

But Alfie wouldn't leave his blanket behind. He held it tightly with one hand, and Bernard's present with the other, all the way to Bernard's house.

When they got there, Bernard's mom opened the door.

"Hello, Alfie," she said. "Let's go into the yard and find Bernard and the others."

Then Mom gave Alfie a kiss and said good-bye, and went off to the park with Annie Rose.

"Would you like to put your blanket down here with the coats?" asked Bernard's mom. But Alfie didn't want to put his blanket down. He still held on to it very tightly.

Bernard was in the back yard with Min and Sam and Daniel and some other children from the nursery school.

"Happy birthday!" Alfie remembered to say, and he gave Bernard his present. Bernard pulled off the paper.

"Crayons! How lovely!" said Bernard's mom. "Say thank you, Bernard."

"Thank you," said Bernard. But do you know what he did then?

He threw the crayons up in the air. They landed all over the grass.

"That was a silly thing to do," said Bernard's mom as she picked up the crayons and put them away.

Then Bernard's mom brought out some bubble stuff and blew lots of bubbles into the air. They floated all over the yard, and the children jumped about trying to pop them.

Alfie couldn't pop many bubbles because he was holding
on to his blanket. But Bernard jumped about and pushed
and popped more bubbles than anyone else.

"Don't push people, Bernard," said Bernard's mom sternly.

One huge bubble landed
lightly on Min's sleeve. It
stayed there, quivering and
shiny. Min smiled. She
stood very still.

Then Bernard came up behind her and popped the big bubble.

Min began to cry. Bernard's mom was cross with Bernard and told him to say he was sorry.

"Never mind, we're going to have something to eat now,
dear," she told Min. "Who would you like to sit next to?"
Min wanted to sit next to Alfie. She stopped crying and
pulled her chair right up close to his.

On the table there were sandwiches and little hot dogs and potato chips and Jell-O and a big cake with candles and "Happy Birthday, Bernard" written on it.

Bernard took a huge breath and blew out all
the candles at once—*Phooooooo!* Everyone clapped
and sang "Happy Birthday to You."

Then Bernard blew into his lemonade through his straw and made rude bubbling noises. He blew into his Jell-O, too, until his mom took it away from him.

Alfie liked everything…but holding on to his blanket made eating rather difficult. It got all mixed up with the Jell-O and potato chips, and covered in sticky crumbs.

When they'd all finished eating, Bernard's mom said that they were all going to play a game. But Bernard ran off and fetched his very best present. It was a tiger mask.

Bernard went behind a bush and came out wearing the mask and making terrible growling noises:
"Grrr! Grrr, grrrr, GRRRR! ACHT!"

He went crawling round the yard, sounding very fierce and frightening.

Min began to cry again. She clung to Alfie.

"Get up *at once*,
Bernard," said
Bernard's mom.
"It's not that kind
of game. Now
let's all stand in a
circle, everyone,
and join hands."

Bernard stopped growling,
but he wouldn't take off
his tiger mask. Instead, he
grabbed Alfie's hand to pull
him into the circle.

Bernard's mom tried to take Min's hand and bring her into the circle too. But Min wouldn't hold anyone's hand but Alfie's. She went on crying. She cried and cried.

Then Alfie made a brave decision. He ran and put down his blanket, very carefully, in a safe place underneath the table.

Now he could hold Min's hand, too, as well as Bernard's.

Min stopped crying. She wasn't
frightened of Bernard in his tiger mask
now that she was holding Alfie's hand.

She joined in the game and they all danced around together, singing:

"Ring-a-ring-o'-roses
A pocket full of posies
A-tishoo, a-tishoo,
We all fall DOWN!"

Afterward Alfie and Min joined in with
some more games and ate ice cream and
popcorn and bounced balloons with the others.
Alfie had such a good time that his blanket
stayed under the table until Mom and Annie
Rose came to collect him.

"What a helpful guest you've been, Alfie," said Bernard's mom, when Alfie thanked her and said good-bye. "Min wouldn't have enjoyed the party a bit without you. I *do* wish Bernard would learn to be helpful sometimes—

—Perhaps he will, one day."

On the way home, Alfie carried his blanket in one hand and a balloon and a bag of candy in the other. His blanket looked a bit messy and it *had* been in the way. Next time he thought he might leave it safely at home, after all.